To lead America into victory in the dark days of World War II, STEVE ROGERS, a scrawny artist from Brooklyn, is injected with a super-soldier formula to become CAPTAIN AMERICA. Fighting against the Axis armies with his devil-may-care partner, BUCKY BARNES, Captain America is the living spirit of the war effort, as his visage alone was enough to inspire greatness and courage in the hearts of every Allied soldier.

Nearing the end of the war, Captain America and Bucky were tasked with guarding an experimental remote-controlled drone bomber. When the drone was commandeered by Nazi agents, Cap and Bucky sprang into action, leaping aboard the drone as it took off. The drone was booby-trapped, however, and in the subsequent explosion Bucky was killed and Cap was thrown to the oceans below.

In suspended animation in the frozen waters for decades, Cap's body was discovered by the modern-day heroes The Avengers. Upon waking, Captain America found himself in an America that was not his own. When the Avengers disappeared, a confused and increasingly desperate Cap struck out alone to discover the truth...and ends up being shot by a young girl he was trying to assist.

CAPTAIN AMERICA:
MAN OUT OF TIME, PART 2

Mark Waid – Writer
Jorge Molina – Pencils & Breakdowns
Karl Kesel – Inks & Finishes
Frank D'Armata – Colorist
VC's Joe Sabino – Letterer & Production
Bryan Hitch, Paul Neary & Paul Mounts – Cover Art
Lauren Sankovitch – Associate Editor
Tom Brevoort – Editor
Joe Quesada – Editor in Chief
Dan Buckley – Publisher
Alan Fine – Executive Producer

Spotlight

MARVEL

visit us at www.abdopublishing.com

Reinforced library bound edition published in 2011 by Spotlight, a division of the ABDO Group, 8000 West 78th Street, Edina, Minnesota 55439. Spotlight produces high-quality reinforced library bound editions for schools and libraries. Published by agreement with Marvel Entertainment, LLC. The stories, characters, and incidents mentioned are entirely fictional.
All rights reserved. Used under authorization.

Printed in the United States of America, Melrose Park, Illinois.
052011
092011
♻ This book contains at least 10% recycled materials.

Library of Congress Cataloging-in-Publication Data

Waid, Mark.
 Man out of time / writer, Mark Waid ; penciler, Jorge Molina.
   v. cm.
 Summary: Frozen in suspended animation for over sixty years, World War II superhero Captain America, aka Steve Rogers, wakes up in the twenty-first century and must adapt to a very changed world.
  ISBN 978-1-59961-936-1 (v. 1) -- ISBN 978-1-59961-937-8 (v. 2) -- ISBN 978-1-59961-938-5 (v. 3) -- ISBN 978-1-59961-939-2 (v. 4) -- ISBN 978-1-59961-940-8 (v. 5)
 1. Graphic novels. [1. Graphic novels. 2. Superheroes--Fiction. 3. Space and time--Fiction.] I. Molina, Jorge, 1984- ill. II. Title.
  PZ7.7.W35Man 2011
  741.5'973--dc22
                            2011013320

All Spotlight books are reinforced library bindings
and manufactured in the United States of America.

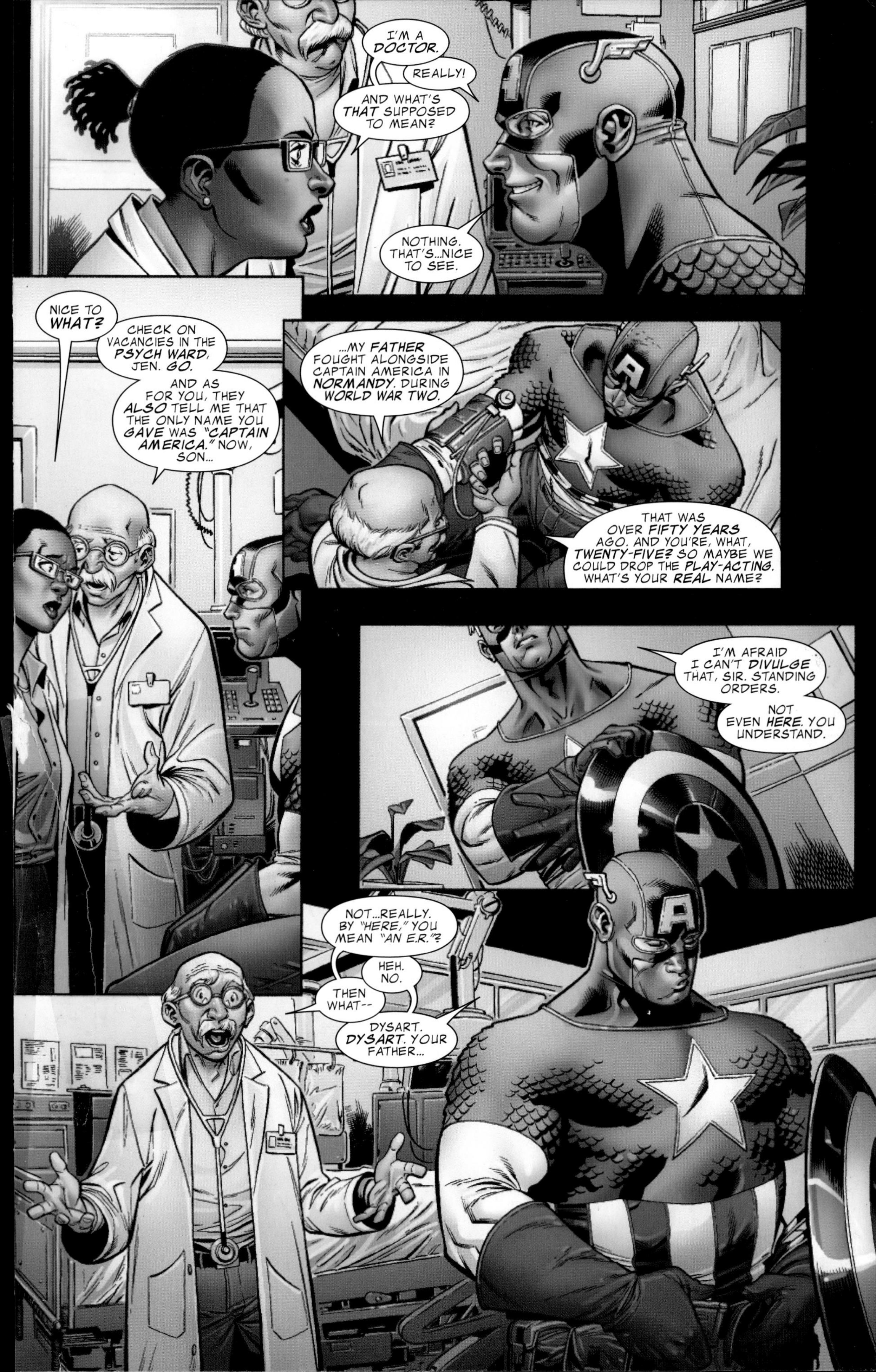
I'M A DOCTOR.
REALLY!
AND WHAT'S THAT SUPPOSED TO MEAN?
NOTHING. THAT'S...NICE TO SEE.
NICE TO WHAT?
CHECK ON VACANCIES IN THE PSYCH WARD, JEN. GO.
AND AS FOR YOU, THEY ALSO TELL ME THAT THE ONLY NAME YOU GAVE WAS "CAPTAIN AMERICA." NOW, SON...
...MY FATHER FOUGHT ALONGSIDE CAPTAIN AMERICA IN NORMANDY. DURING WORLD WAR TWO.
THAT WAS OVER FIFTY YEARS AGO. AND YOU'RE, WHAT, TWENTY-FIVE? SO MAYBE WE COULD DROP THE PLAY-ACTING. WHAT'S YOUR REAL NAME?
I'M AFRAID I CAN'T DIVULGE THAT, SIR. STANDING ORDERS.
NOT EVEN HERE. YOU UNDERSTAND.
NOT...REALLY. BY "HERE," YOU MEAN "AN E.R."?
HEH. NO.
THEN WHAT--
DYSART. DYSART. YOUR FATHER...

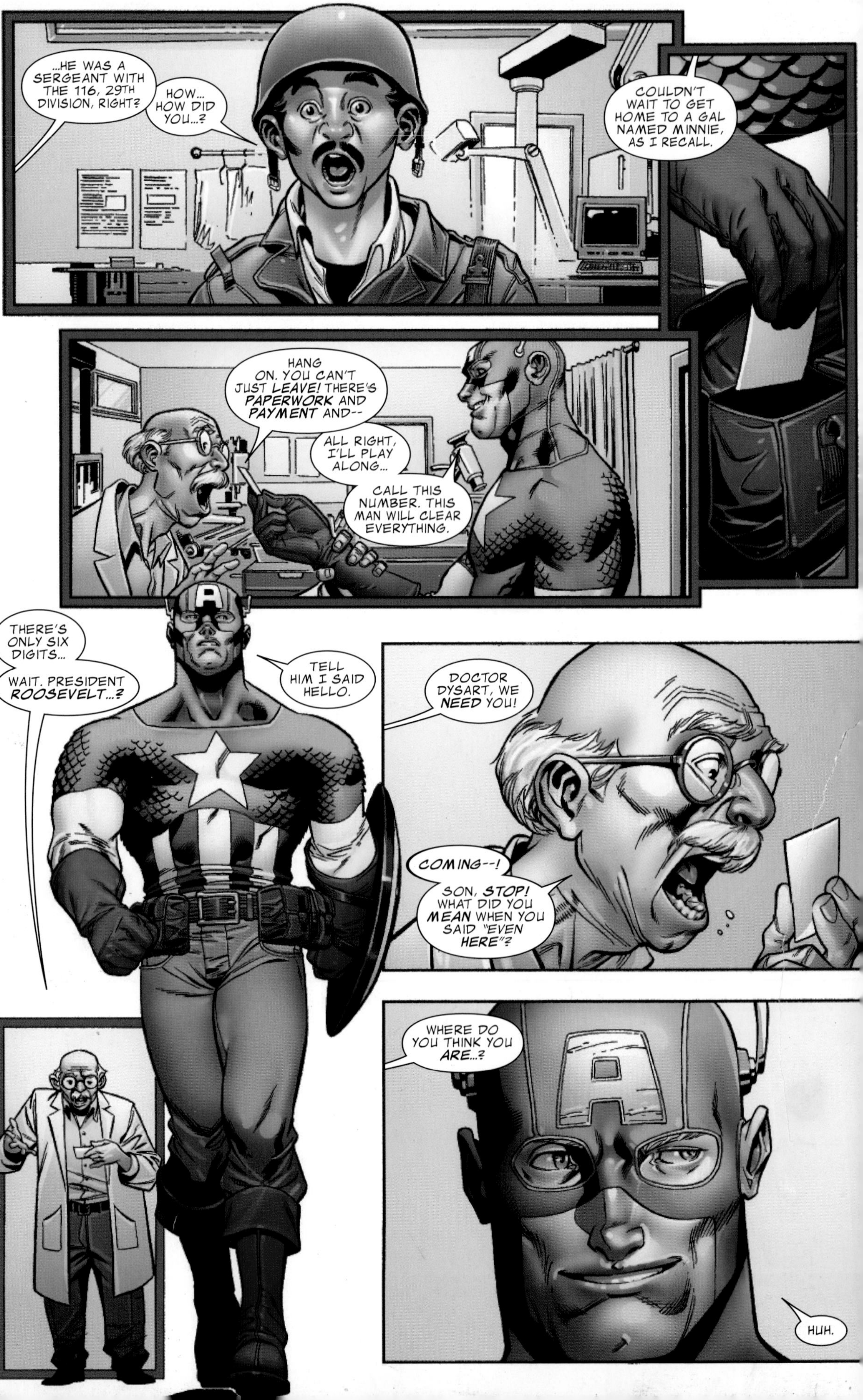
...HE WAS A SERGEANT WITH THE 116, 29TH DIVISION, RIGHT?
HOW... HOW DID YOU...?
COULDN'T WAIT TO GET HOME TO A GAL NAMED MINNIE, AS I RECALL.
HANG ON. YOU CAN'T JUST LEAVE! THERE'S PAPERWORK AND PAYMENT AND--
ALL RIGHT, I'LL PLAY ALONG...
CALL THIS NUMBER. THIS MAN WILL CLEAR EVERYTHING.
THERE'S ONLY SIX DIGITS...
WAIT. PRESIDENT ROOSEVELT...?
TELL HIM I SAID HELLO.
DOCTOR DYSART, WE NEED YOU!
COMING--!
SON, STOP! WHAT DID YOU MEAN WHEN YOU SAID "EVEN HERE"?
WHERE DO YOU THINK YOU ARE...?
HUH.

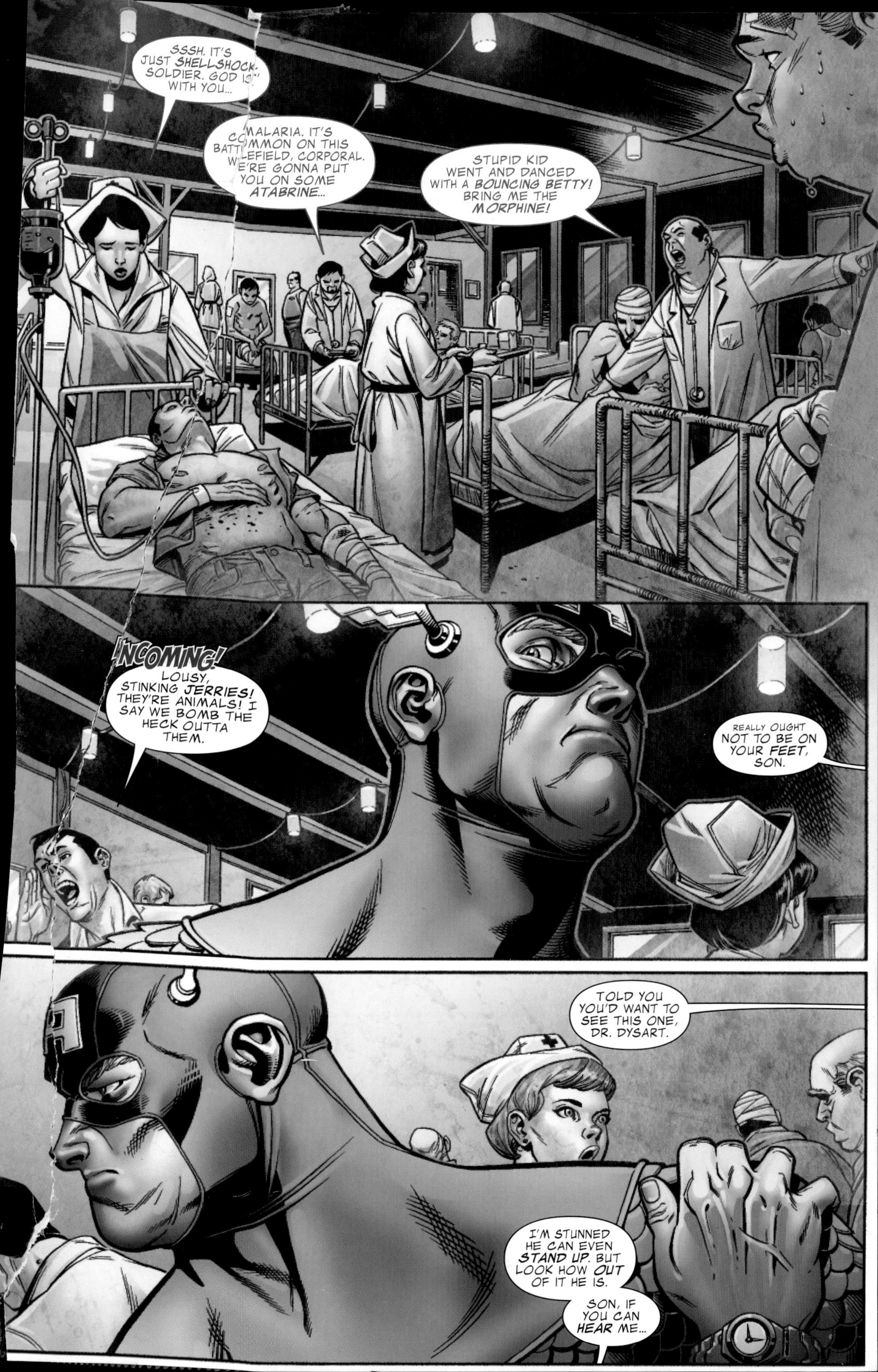
SSSH. IT'S JUST SHELLSHOCK, SOLDIER. GOD IS WITH YOU...
MALARIA. IT'S COMMON ON THIS BATTLEFIELD, CORPORAL. WE'RE GONNA PUT YOU ON SOME ATABRINE...
STUPID KID WENT AND DANCED WITH A BOUNCING BETTY! BRING ME THE MORPHINE!
INCOMING!
LOUSY, STINKING JERRIES! THEY'RE ANIMALS! I SAY WE BOMB THE HECK OUTTA THEM.
REALLY OUGHT NOT TO BE ON YOUR FEET, SON.
TOLD YOU YOU'D WANT TO SEE THIS ONE, DR. DYSART.
I'M STUNNED HE CAN EVEN STAND UP. BUT LOOK HOW OUT OF IT HE IS.
SON, IF YOU CAN HEAR ME...

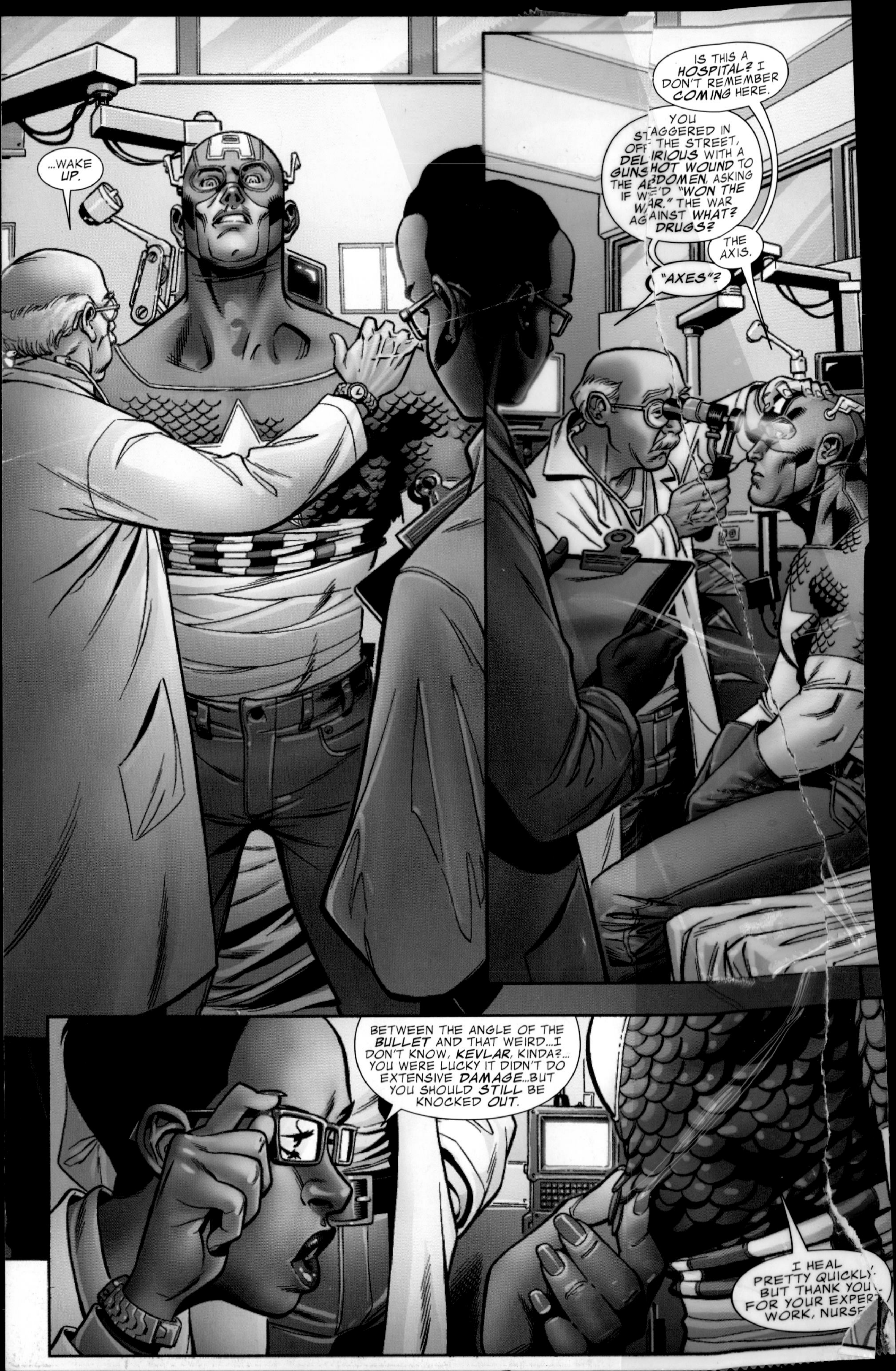
...WAKE UP.
IS THIS A HOSPITAL? I DON'T REMEMBER COMING HERE.
YOU STAGGERED IN OFF THE STREET, DELIRIOUS WITH A GUNSHOT WOUND TO THE ABDOMEN, ASKING IF WE'D "WON THE WAR." THE WAR AGAINST WHAT? DRUGS?
THE AXIS.
"AXES"?
BETWEEN THE ANGLE OF THE BULLET AND THAT WEIRD...I DON'T KNOW, KEVLAR, KINDA?... YOU WERE LUCKY IT DIDN'T DO EXTENSIVE DAMAGE...BUT YOU SHOULD STILL BE KNOCKED OUT.
I HEAL PRETTY QUICKLY. BUT THANK YOU FOR YOUR EXPERT WORK, NURSE

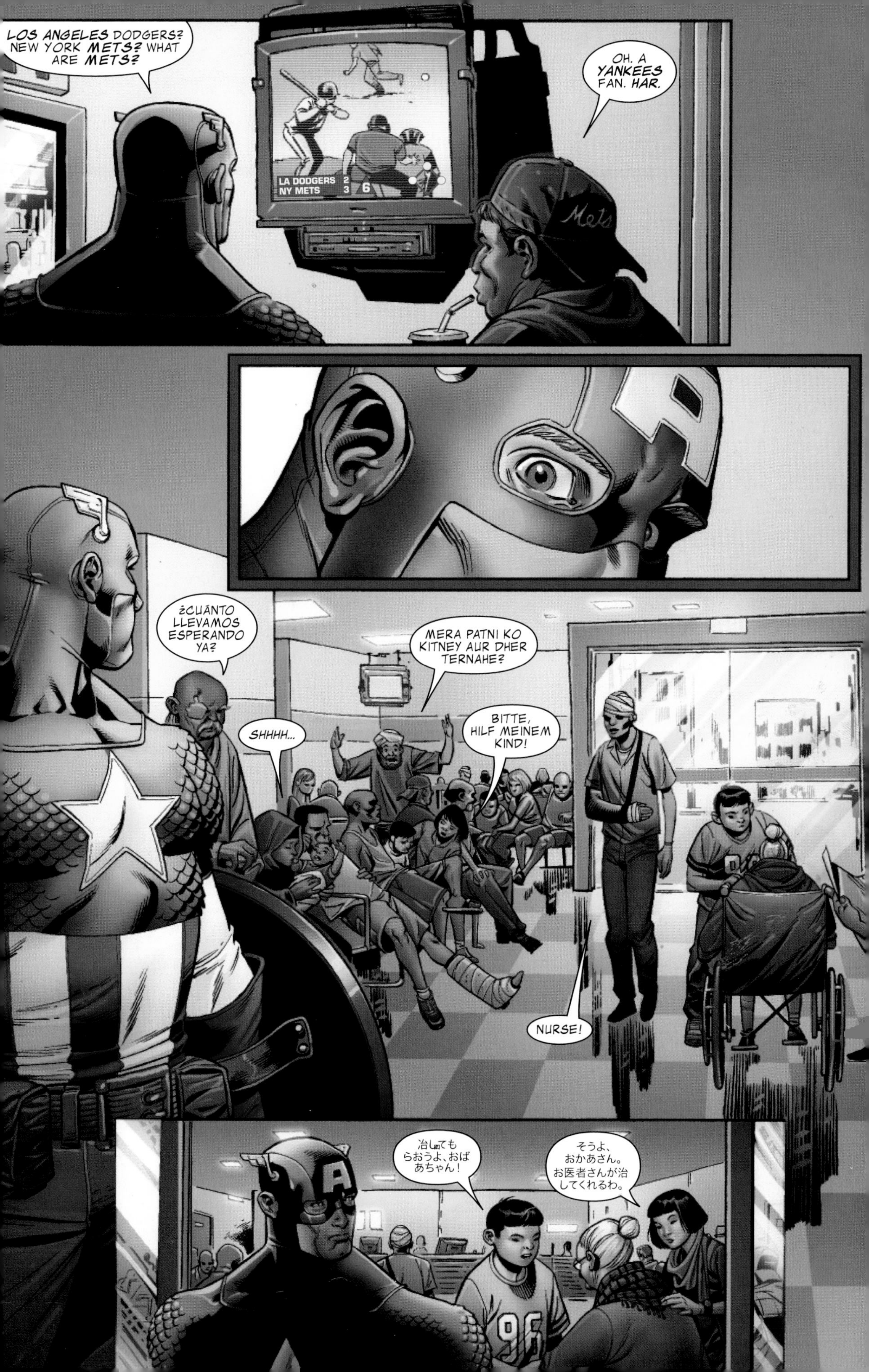
LOS ANGELES DODGERS? NEW YORK METS? WHAT ARE METS?
LA DODGERS 2
NY METS 3 6
Mets
OH. A YANKEES FAN. HAR.
¿CUÁNTO LLEVAMOS ESPERANDO YA?
MERA PATNI KO KITNEY AUR DHER TERNAHE?
SHHHH...
BITTE, HILF MEINEM KIND!
NURSE!
治してもらおうよ、おばあちゃん！
そうよ、おかあさん。お医者さんが治してくれるわ。

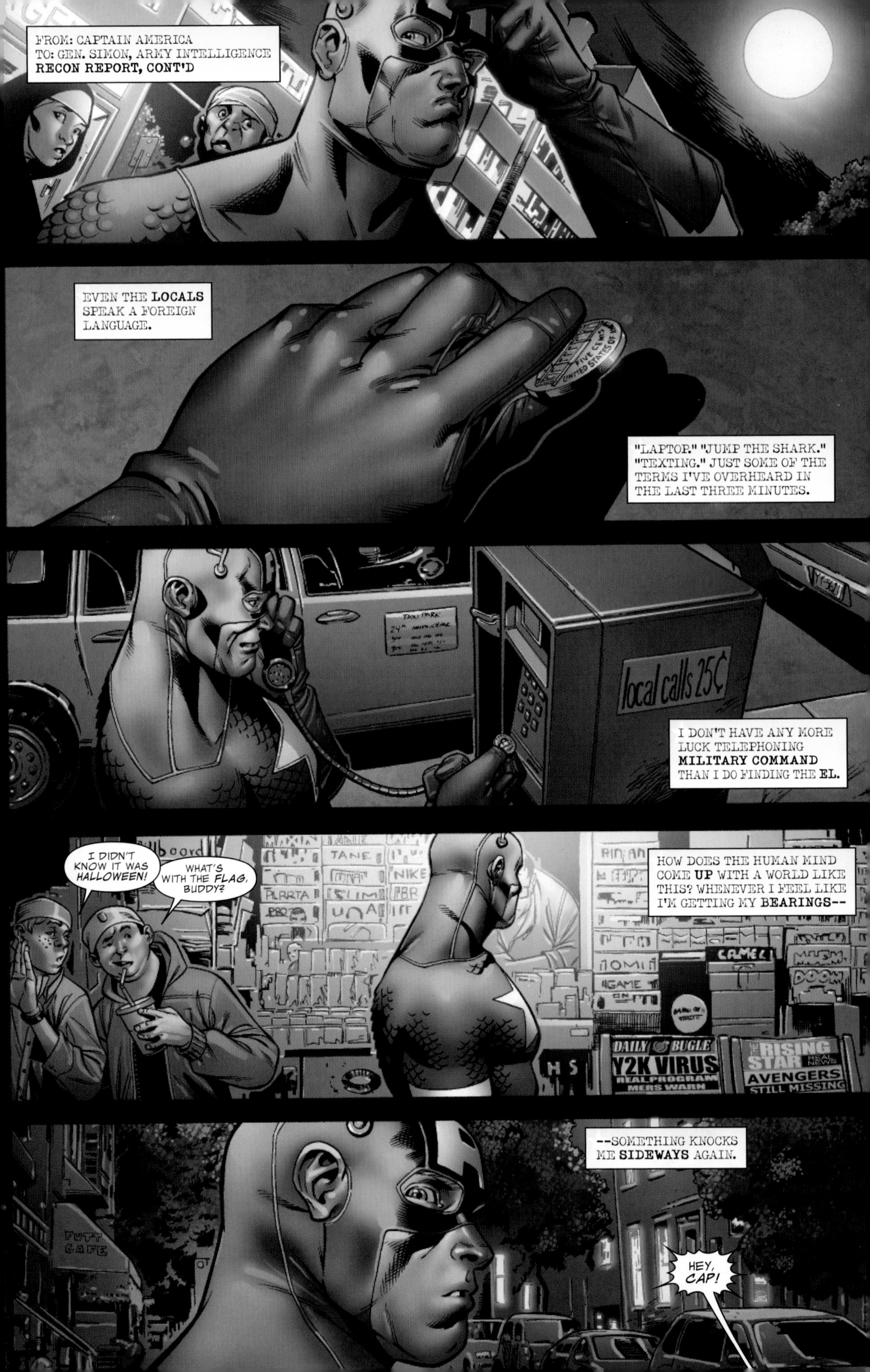

FROM: CAPTAIN AMERICA
TO: GEN. SIMON, ARMY INTELLIGENCE
RECON REPORT, CONT'D
EVEN THE LOCALS SPEAK A FOREIGN LANGUAGE.
FIVE CENTS
UNITED STATES OF
"LAPTOP." "JUMP THE SHARK." "TEXTING." JUST SOME OF THE TERMS I'VE OVERHEARD IN THE LAST THREE MINUTES.
local calls 25¢
I DON'T HAVE ANY MORE LUCK TELEPHONING MILITARY COMMAND THAN I DO FINDING THE EL.
I DIDN'T KNOW IT WAS HALLOWEEN!
WHAT'S WITH THE FLAG, BUDDY?
HOW DOES THE HUMAN MIND COME UP WITH A WORLD LIKE THIS? WHENEVER I FEEL LIKE I'M GETTING MY BEARINGS--
NIKE
CAMEL
DOOM
DAILY BUGLE
Y2K VIRUS
REALPROGRAM MERS WARN
THE RISING STAR
REAL NEWS
AVENGERS STILL MISSING
--SOMETHING KNOCKS ME SIDEWAYS AGAIN.
CAFE
HEY, CAP!

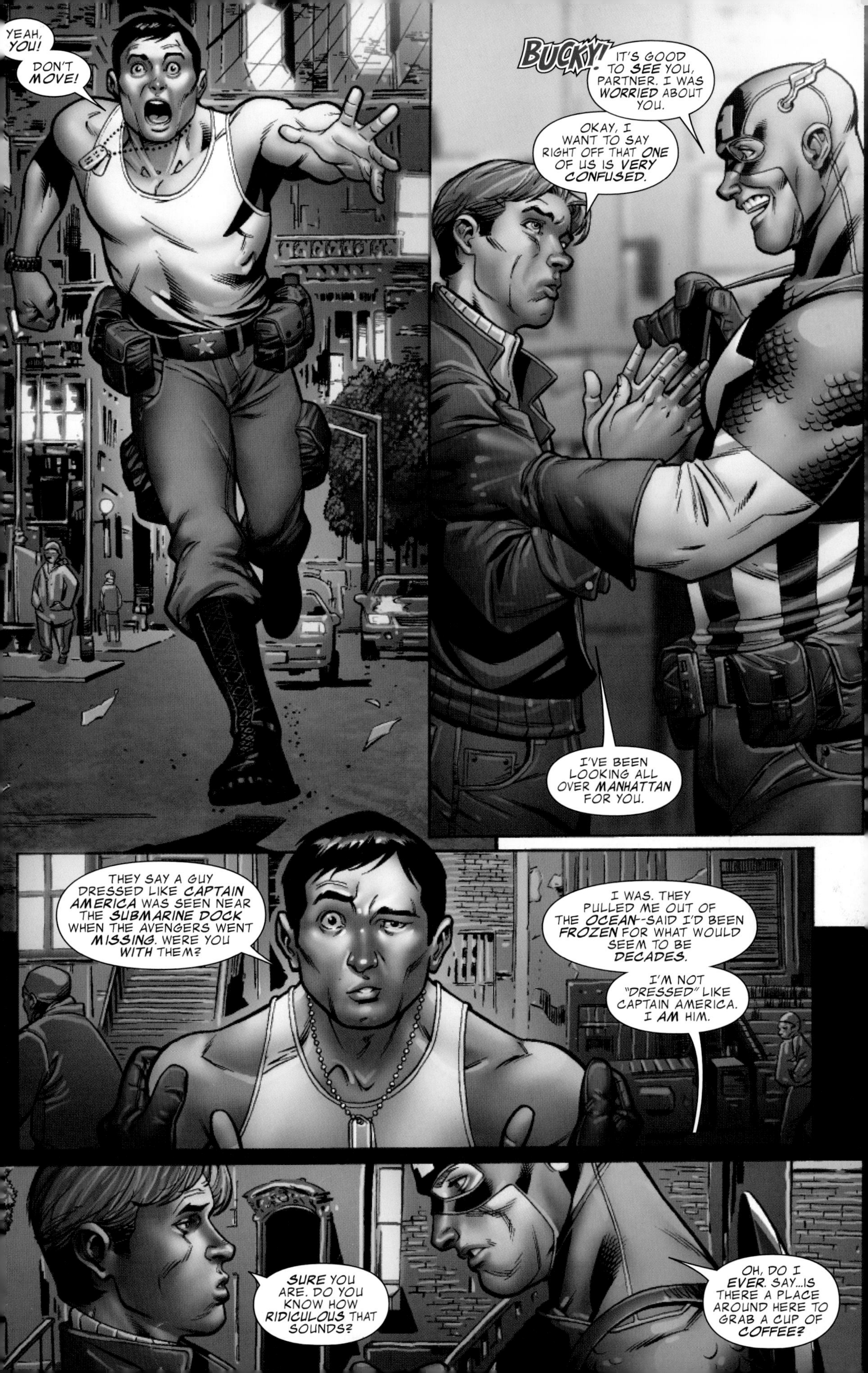
YEAH, YOU!
DON'T MOVE!
BUCKY!
IT'S GOOD TO SEE YOU, PARTNER. I WAS WORRIED ABOUT YOU.
OKAY, I WANT TO SAY RIGHT OFF THAT ONE OF US IS VERY CONFUSED.
I'VE BEEN LOOKING ALL OVER MANHATTAN FOR YOU.
THEY SAY A GUY DRESSED LIKE CAPTAIN AMERICA WAS SEEN NEAR THE SUBMARINE DOCK WHEN THE AVENGERS WENT MISSING. WERE YOU WITH THEM?
I WAS. THEY PULLED ME OUT OF THE OCEAN--SAID I'D BEEN FROZEN FOR WHAT WOULD SEEM TO BE DECADES.
I'M NOT "DRESSED" LIKE CAPTAIN AMERICA. I AM HIM.
SURE YOU ARE. DO YOU KNOW HOW RIDICULOUS THAT SOUNDS?
OH, DO I EVER. SAY...IS THERE A PLACE AROUND HERE TO GRAB A CUP OF COFFEE?

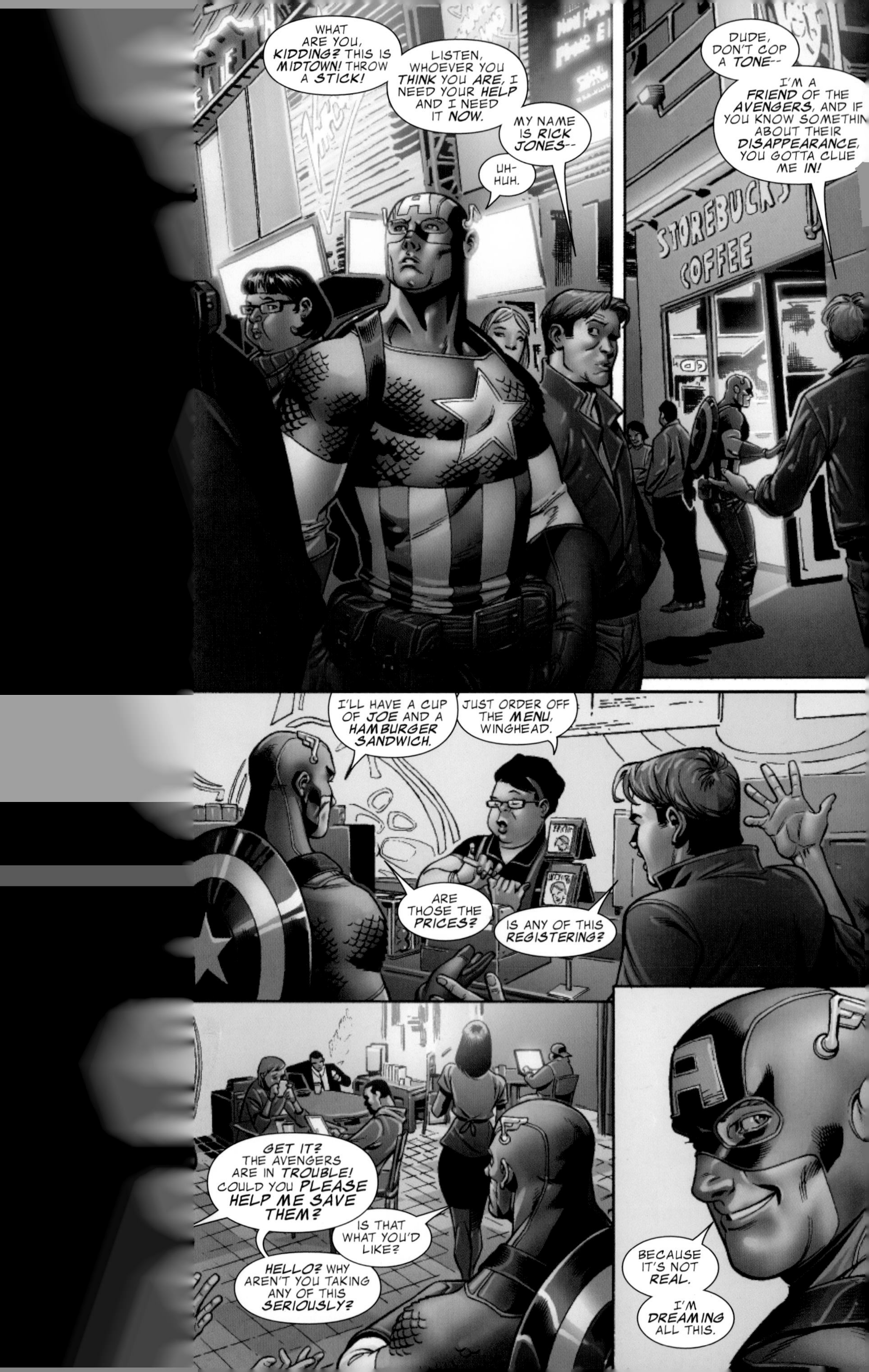
WHAT ARE YOU, KIDDING? THIS IS MIDTOWN! THROW A STICK!
LISTEN, WHOEVER YOU THINK YOU ARE, I NEED YOUR HELP AND I NEED IT NOW.
MY NAME IS RICK JONES--
UH-HUH.
DUDE, DON'T COP A TONE--
I'M A FRIEND OF THE AVENGERS, AND IF YOU KNOW SOMETHIN ABOUT THEIR DISAPPEARANCE, YOU GOTTA CLUE ME IN!
STOREBUCKS COFFEE
I'LL HAVE A CUP OF JOE AND A HAMBURGER SANDWICH.
JUST ORDER OFF THE MENU, WINGHEAD.
ARE THOSE THE PRICES?
IS ANY OF THIS REGISTERING?
GET IT? THE AVENGERS ARE IN TROUBLE! COULD YOU PLEASE HELP ME SAVE THEM?
IS THAT WHAT YOU'D LIKE?
HELLO? WHY AREN'T YOU TAKING ANY OF THIS SERIOUSLY?
BECAUSE IT'S NOT REAL.
I'M DREAMING ALL THIS.

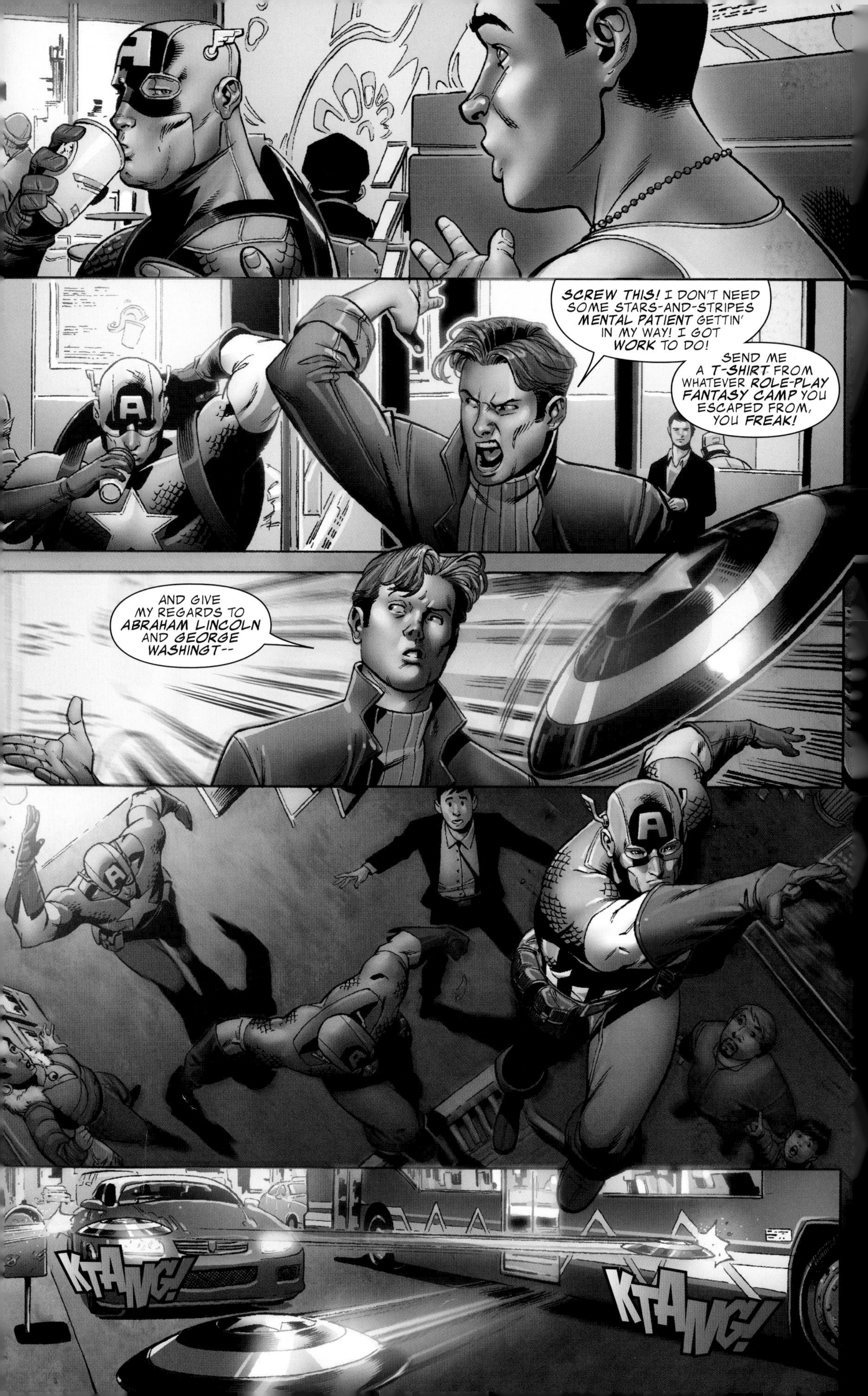
SCREW THIS! I DON'T NEED SOME STARS-AND-STRIPES MENTAL PATIENT GETTIN' IN MY WAY! I GOT WORK TO DO!
SEND ME A T-SHIRT FROM WHATEVER ROLE-PLAY FANTASY CAMP YOU ESCAPED FROM, YOU FREAK!
AND GIVE MY REGARDS TO ABRAHAM LINCOLN AND GEORGE WASHINGT--
KTANG!
KTANG!

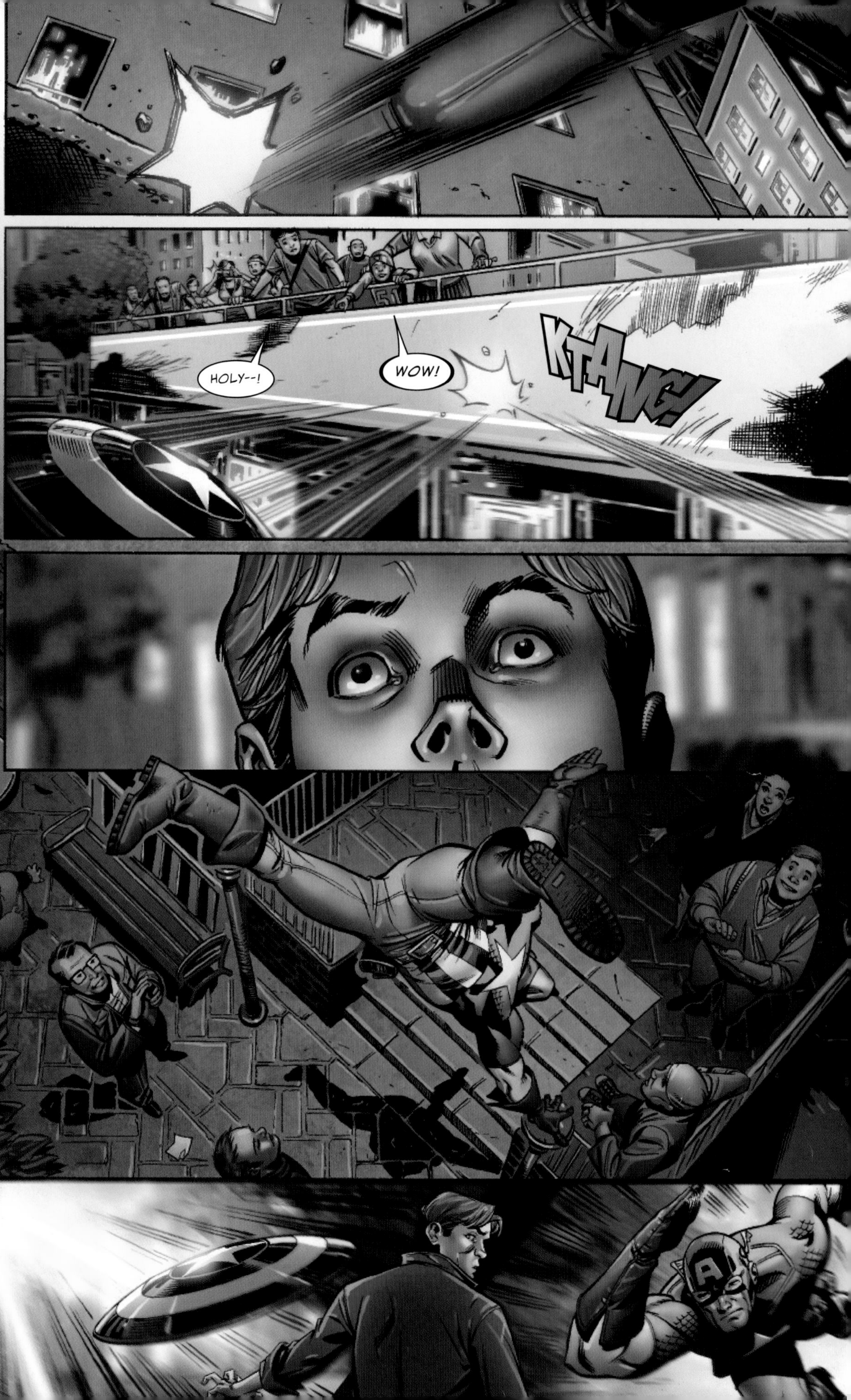
HOLY--!
WOW!
KTANG!

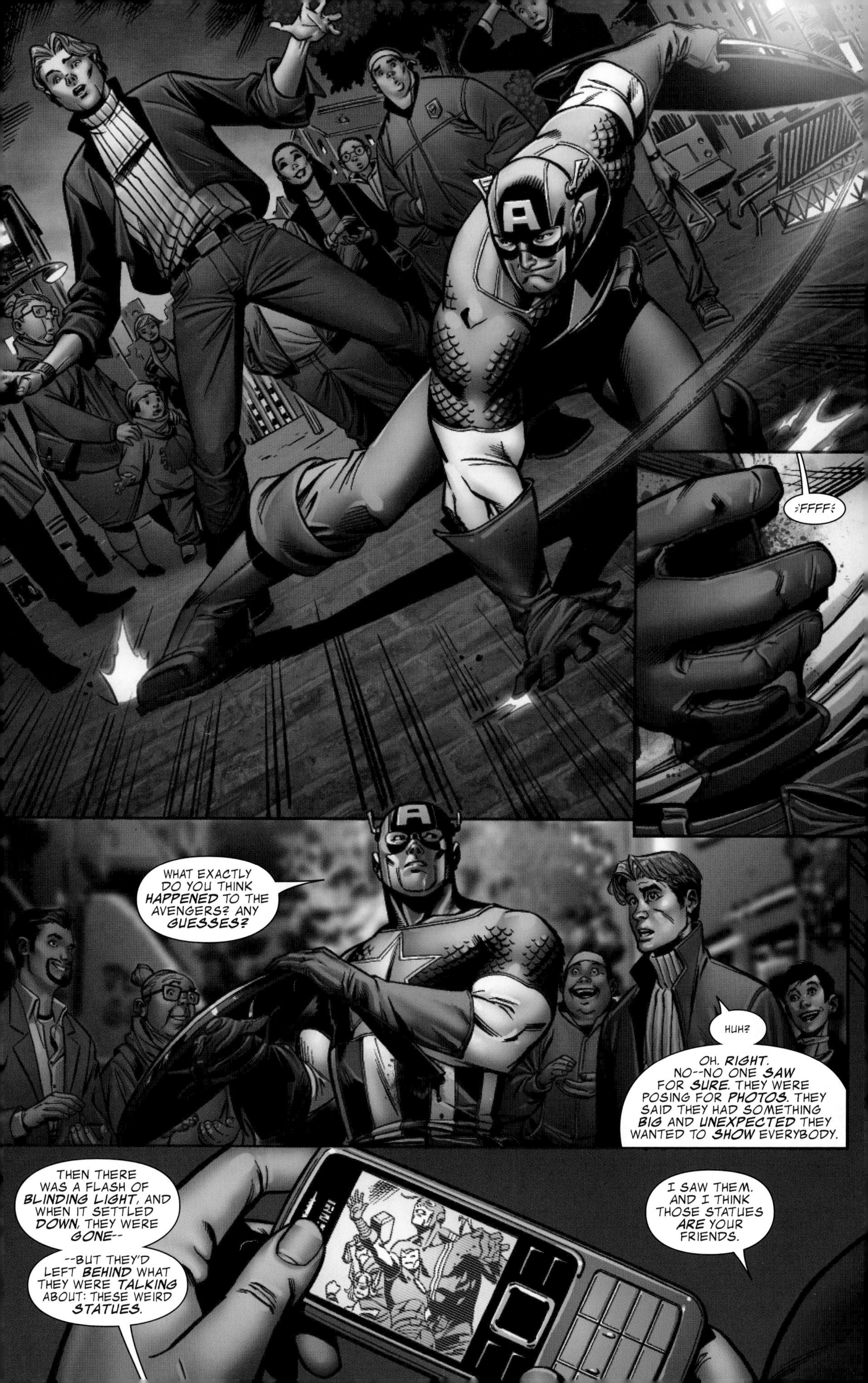

FFFF
WHAT EXACTLY DO YOU THINK HAPPENED TO THE AVENGERS? ANY GUESSES?
HUH?
OH. RIGHT. NO--NO ONE SAW FOR SURE. THEY WERE POSING FOR PHOTOS. THEY SAID THEY HAD SOMETHING BIG AND UNEXPECTED THEY WANTED TO SHOW EVERYBODY.
THEN THERE WAS A FLASH OF BLINDING LIGHT, AND WHEN IT SETTLED DOWN, THEY WERE GONE--
--BUT THEY'D LEFT BEHIND WHAT THEY WERE TALKING ABOUT: THESE WEIRD STATUES.
I SAW THEM. AND I THINK THOSE STATUES ARE YOUR FRIENDS.

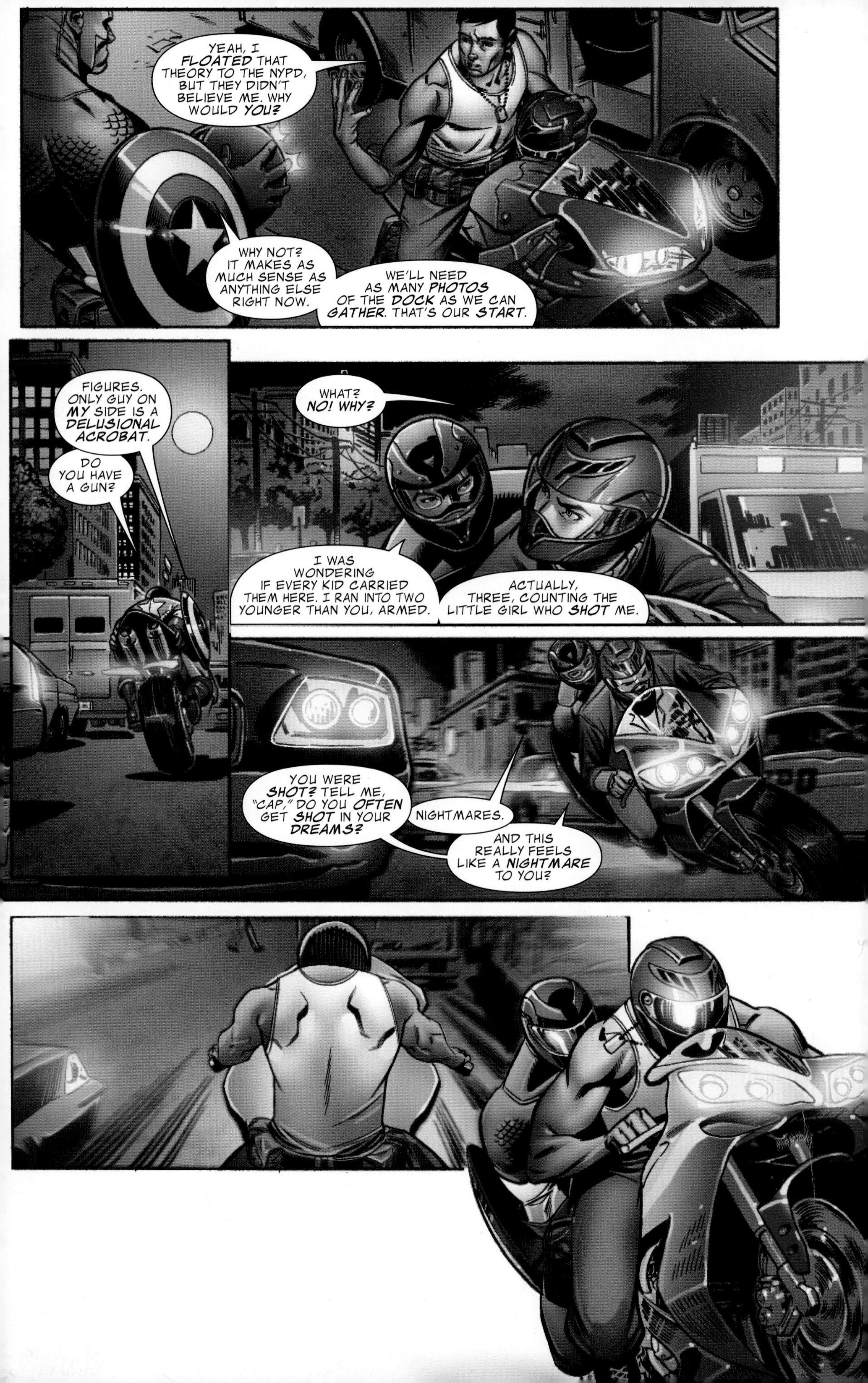
YEAH, I FLOATED THAT THEORY TO THE NYPD, BUT THEY DIDN'T BELIEVE ME. WHY WOULD YOU?
WHY NOT? IT MAKES AS MUCH SENSE AS ANYTHING ELSE RIGHT NOW.
WE'LL NEED AS MANY PHOTOS OF THE DOCK AS WE CAN GATHER. THAT'S OUR START.
FIGURES. ONLY GUY ON MY SIDE IS A DELUSIONAL ACROBAT.
DO YOU HAVE A GUN?
WHAT? NO! WHY?
I WAS WONDERING IF EVERY KID CARRIED THEM HERE. I RAN INTO TWO YOUNGER THAN YOU, ARMED.
ACTUALLY, THREE, COUNTING THE LITTLE GIRL WHO SHOT ME.
YOU WERE SHOT? TELL ME, "CAP," DO YOU OFTEN GET SHOT IN YOUR DREAMS?
NIGHTMARES.
AND THIS REALLY FEELS LIKE A NIGHTMARE TO YOU?

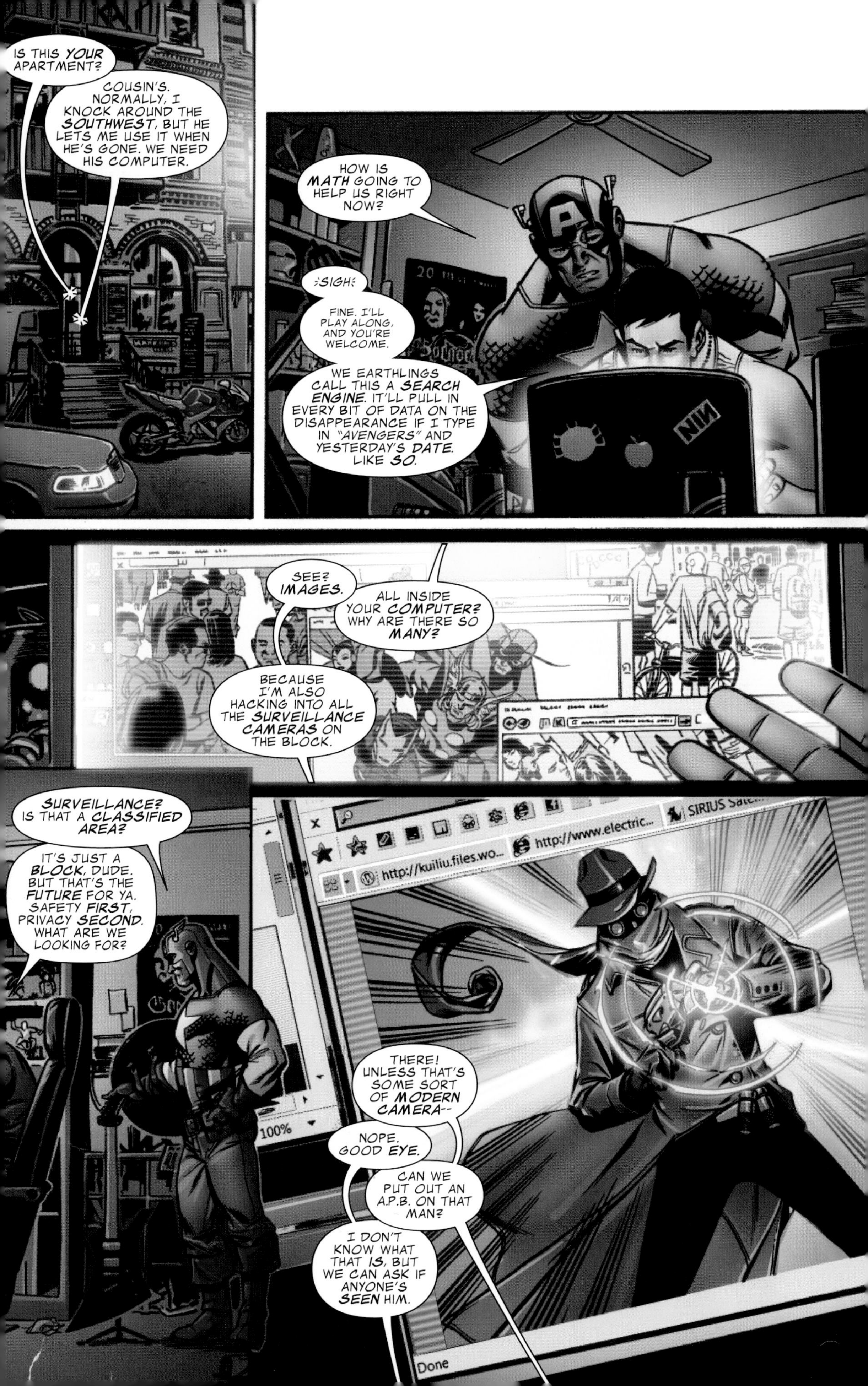
IS THIS YOUR APARTMENT?
COUSIN'S. NORMALLY, I KNOCK AROUND THE SOUTHWEST, BUT HE LETS ME USE IT WHEN HE'S GONE. WE NEED HIS COMPUTER.
HOW IS MATH GOING TO HELP US RIGHT NOW?
:SIGH:
FINE. I'LL PLAY ALONG, AND YOU'RE WELCOME.
WE EARTHLINGS CALL THIS A SEARCH ENGINE. IT'LL PULL IN EVERY BIT OF DATA ON THE DISAPPEARANCE IF I TYPE IN "AVENGERS" AND YESTERDAY'S DATE. LIKE SO.
NIN
SEE? IMAGES.
ALL INSIDE YOUR COMPUTER? WHY ARE THERE SO MANY?
BECAUSE I'M ALSO HACKING INTO ALL THE SURVEILLANCE CAMERAS ON THE BLOCK.
SURVEILLANCE? IS THAT A CLASSIFIED AREA?
IT'S JUST A BLOCK, DUDE. BUT THAT'S THE FUTURE FOR YA. SAFETY FIRST, PRIVACY SECOND. WHAT ARE WE LOOKING FOR?
SIRIUS Sate...
http://www.electric...
http://kuiliu.files.wo...
100%
THERE! UNLESS THAT'S SOME SORT OF MODERN CAMERA--
NOPE. GOOD EYE.
CAN WE PUT OUT AN A.P.B. ON THAT MAN?
I DON'T KNOW WHAT THAT IS, BUT WE CAN ASK IF ANYONE'S SEEN HIM.
Done

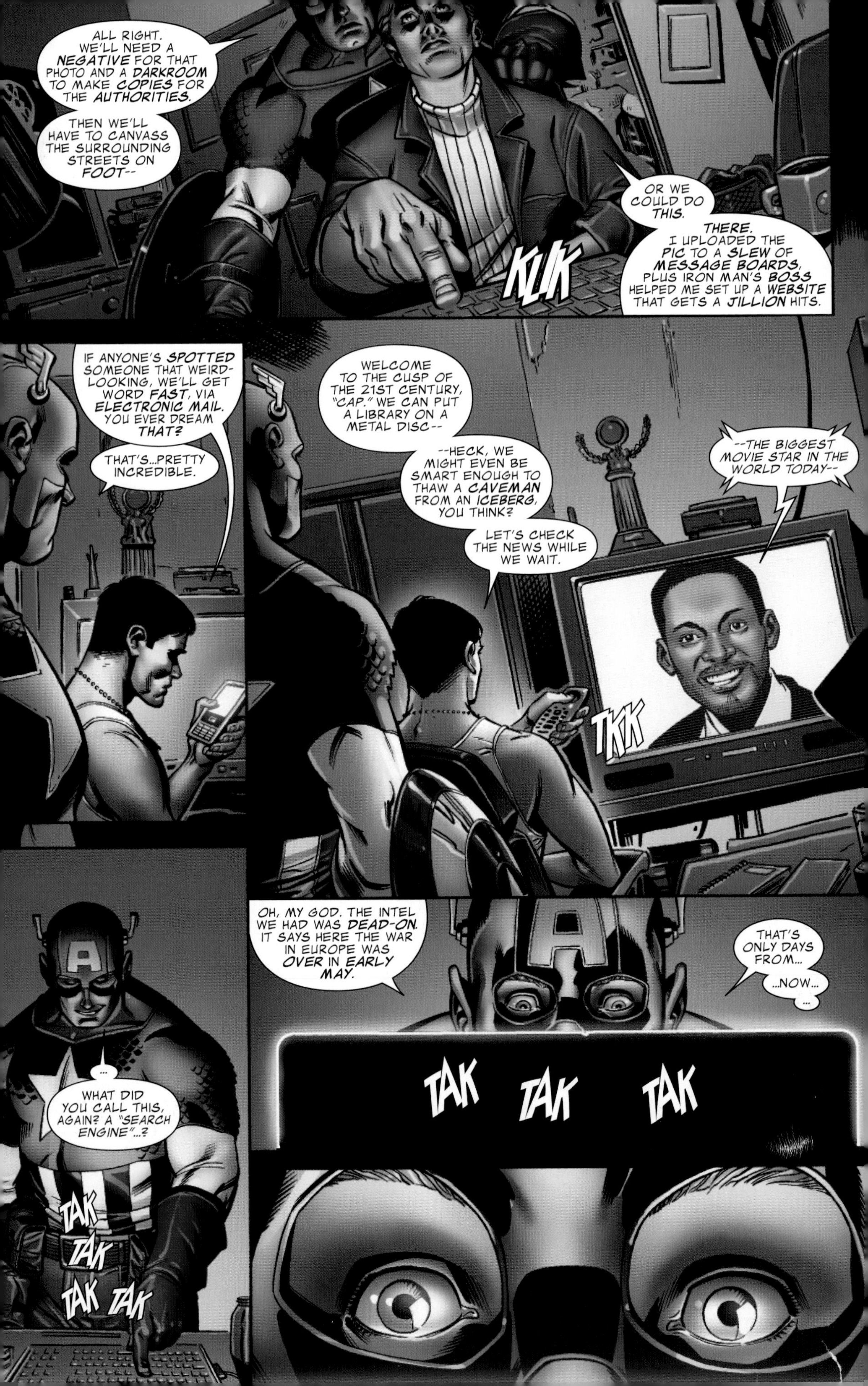
ALL RIGHT. WE'LL NEED A NEGATIVE FOR THAT PHOTO AND A DARKROOM TO MAKE COPIES FOR THE AUTHORITIES.
THEN WE'LL HAVE TO CANVASS THE SURROUNDING STREETS ON FOOT--
OR WE COULD DO THIS.
KLIK
THERE. I UPLOADED THE PIC TO A SLEW OF MESSAGE BOARDS, PLUS IRON MAN'S BOSS HELPED ME SET UP A WEBSITE THAT GETS A JILLION HITS.
IF ANYONE'S SPOTTED SOMEONE THAT WEIRD-LOOKING, WE'LL GET WORD FAST, VIA ELECTRONIC MAIL. YOU EVER DREAM THAT?
THAT'S...PRETTY INCREDIBLE.
WELCOME TO THE CUSP OF THE 21ST CENTURY, "CAP." WE CAN PUT A LIBRARY ON A METAL DISC--
--HECK, WE MIGHT EVEN BE SMART ENOUGH TO THAW A CAVEMAN FROM AN ICEBERG, YOU THINK?
LET'S CHECK THE NEWS WHILE WE WAIT.
TKK
--THE BIGGEST MOVIE STAR IN THE WORLD TODAY--
...
WHAT DID YOU CALL THIS, AGAIN? A "SEARCH ENGINE"...?
TAK TAK TAK TAK
OH, MY GOD. THE INTEL WE HAD WAS DEAD-ON. IT SAYS HERE THE WAR IN EUROPE WAS OVER IN EARLY MAY.
THAT'S ONLY DAYS FROM...
...NOW...
...
TAK TAK TAK

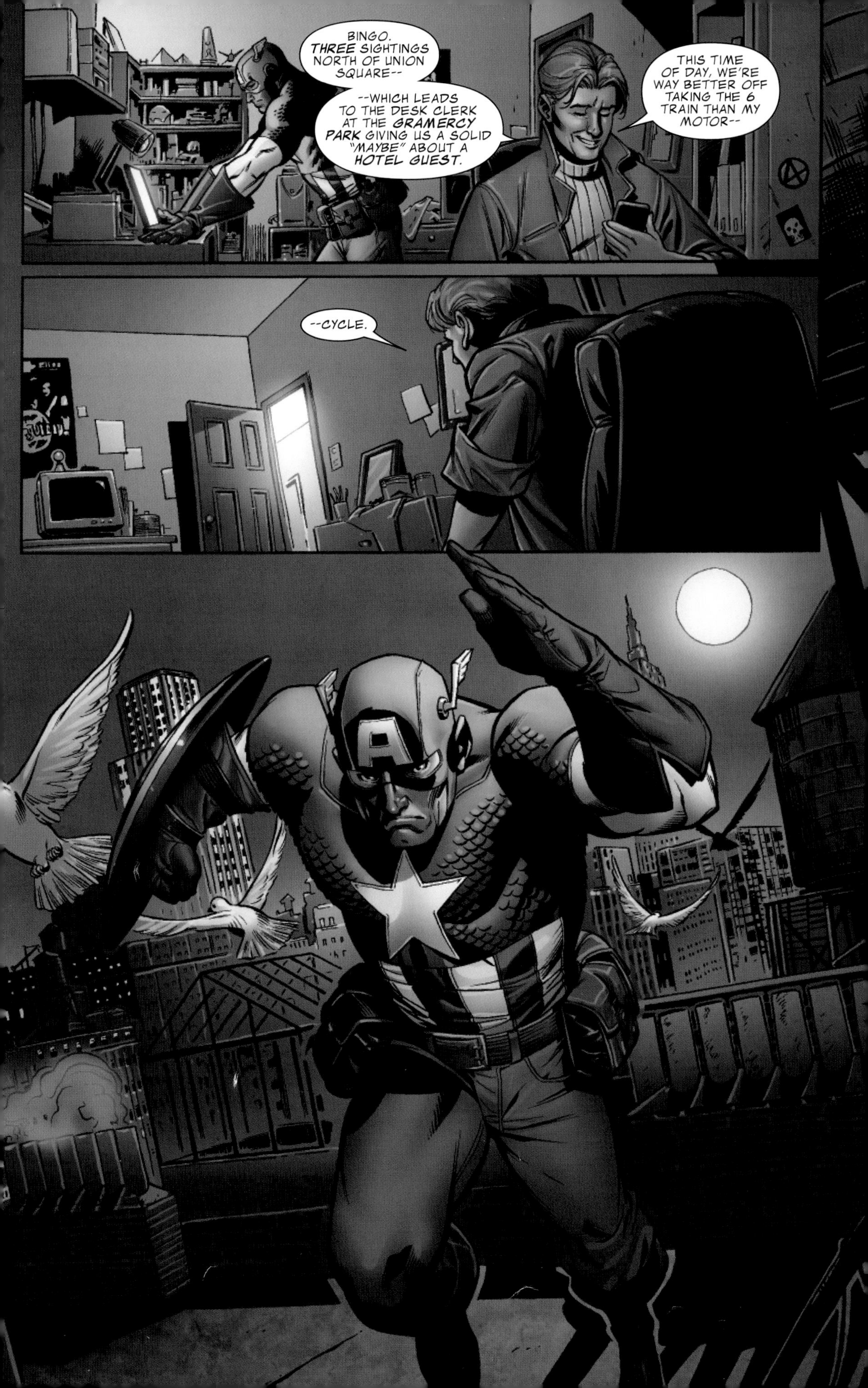
BINGO. THREE SIGHTINGS NORTH OF UNION SQUARE--
--WHICH LEADS TO THE DESK CLERK AT THE GRAMERCY PARK GIVING US A SOLID "MAYBE" ABOUT A HOTEL GUEST.
THIS TIME OF DAY, WE'RE WAY BETTER OFF TAKING THE 6 TRAIN THAN MY MOTOR--
--CYCLE.

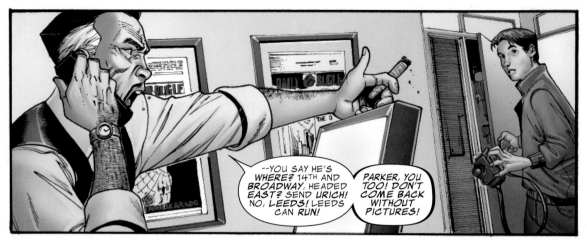

--YOU SAY HE'S WHERE? 14TH AND BROADWAY, HEADED EAST? SEND URICH! NO, LEEDS! LEEDS CAN RUN!

PARKER, YOU TOO! DON'T COME BACK WITHOUT PICTURES!

--WHERE, JUST HOURS AGO, LOCAL ACTIVISTS PROTESTED--

--WAIT! FORGET ME, GET HIM! GET THE SHOT! LADIES AND GENTLEMEN--

--YOU'RE SEEING LIVE FOOTAGE OF THE MYSTERY MAN WHO JUST HOURS AGO BROUGHT MIDTOWN TO A STANDSTILL WITH A SUPERHUMAN DISPLAY OF ACROBATICS!

IS HE AN ACTOR? IS THIS A PUBLICITY STUNT OF SOME KIND? OR IS THERE A NEW HERO ON THE SCENE?

NO ONE AUTHORIZED THIS, MR. PRESIDENT. WHOEVER HE IS, HE'S A WILD CARD, BUT OUR BEST MEN ARE ALREADY ON IT. WE WILL GET ANSWERS.

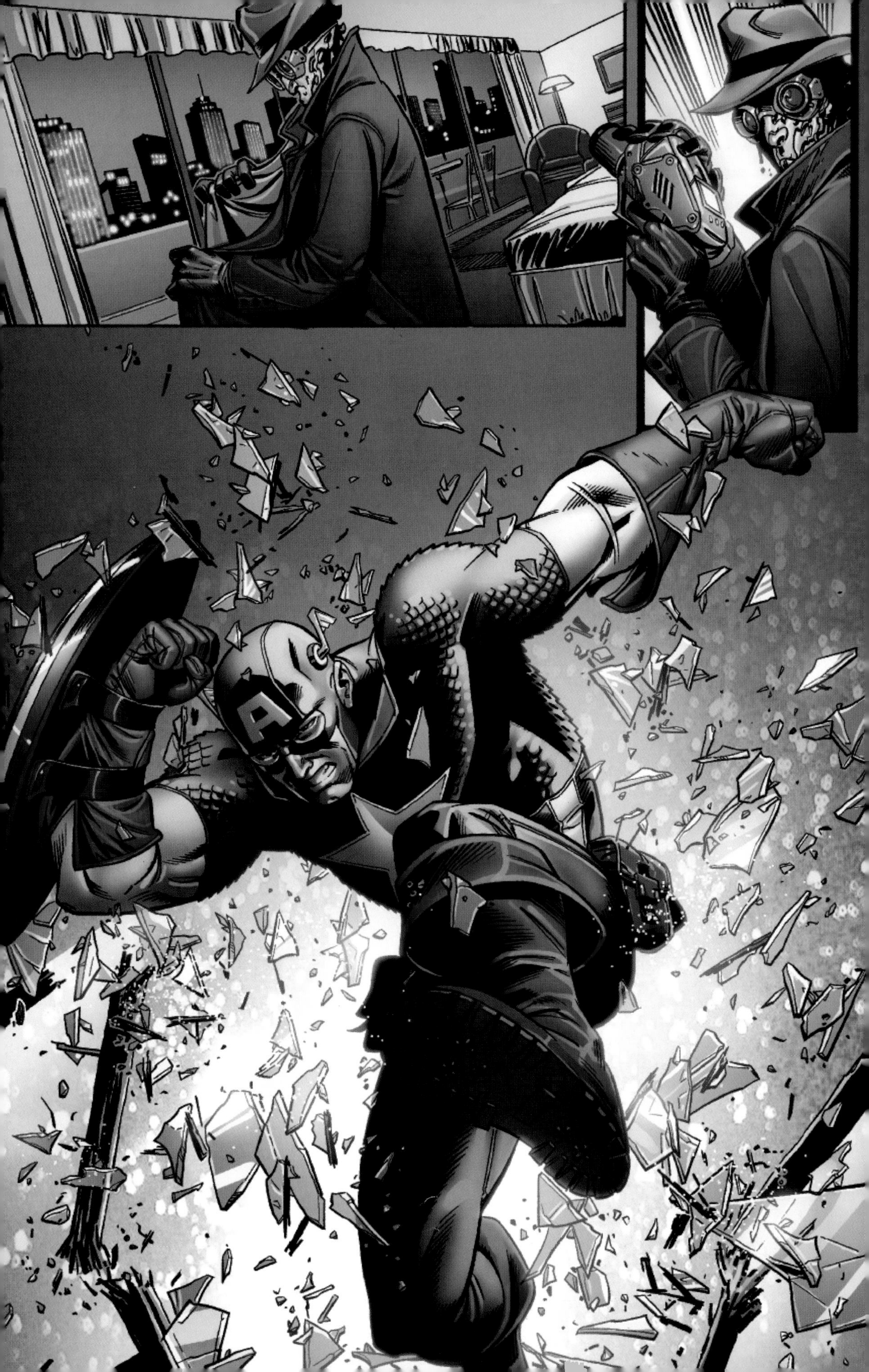

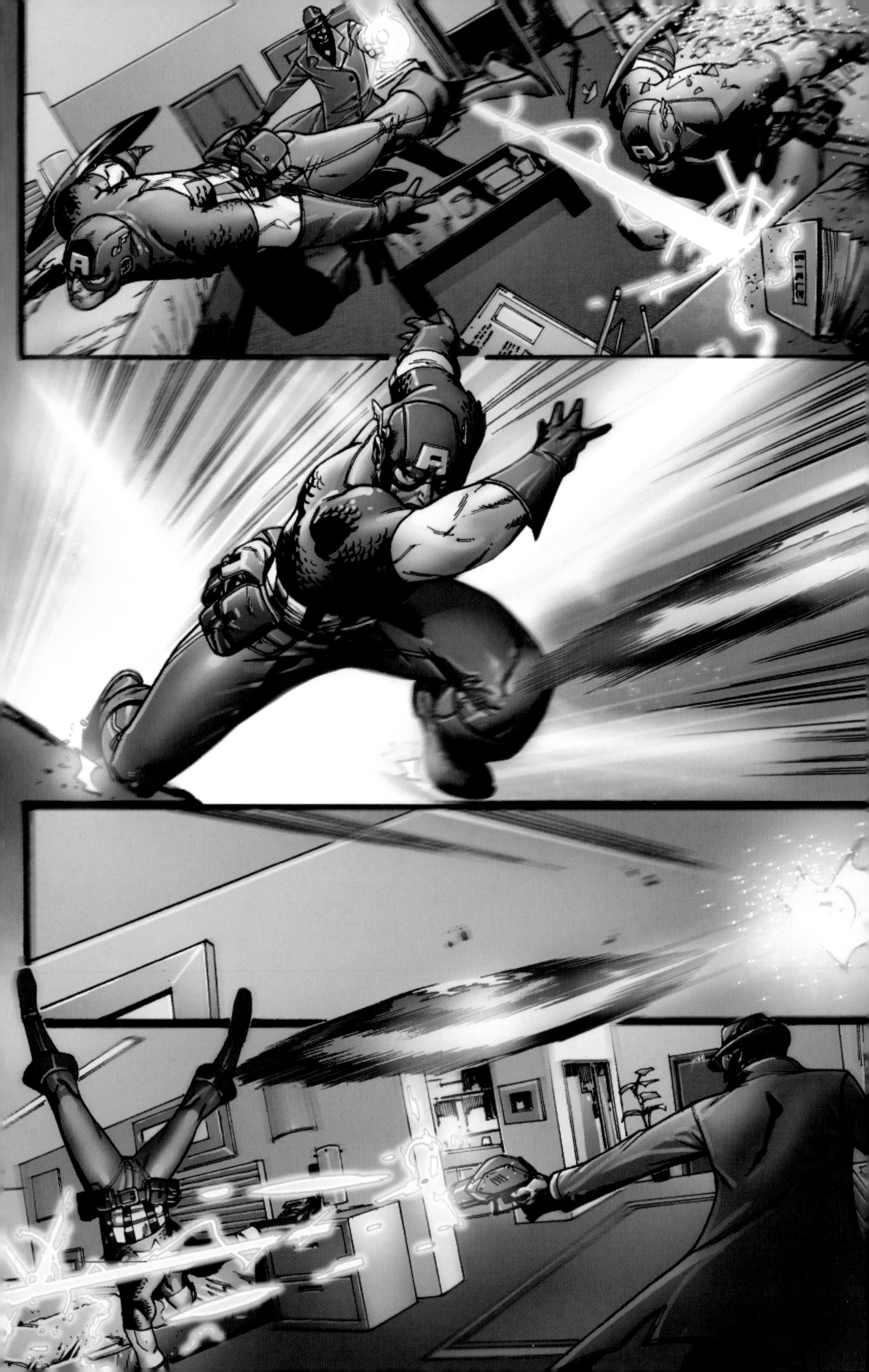

WHO ARE YOU? **TALK!**

SMÏÄÆ NÏGGLÏEM

SMÏÄÆ NÏGGLÏEM

I ÆSÆ **REVERSE**. NO **HURT**. WÆNÄ CAN **REVERSE** RAY--!

HEH.

YOU'RE A **MAN FROM MARS.**

OF **COURSE** YOU'RE A MAN FROM MARS!

AHAHAHAHAHAHAHAHAHAHAH
AHAHAHAHAHAHAHAHAHAHAH
AHAHAHAHAH

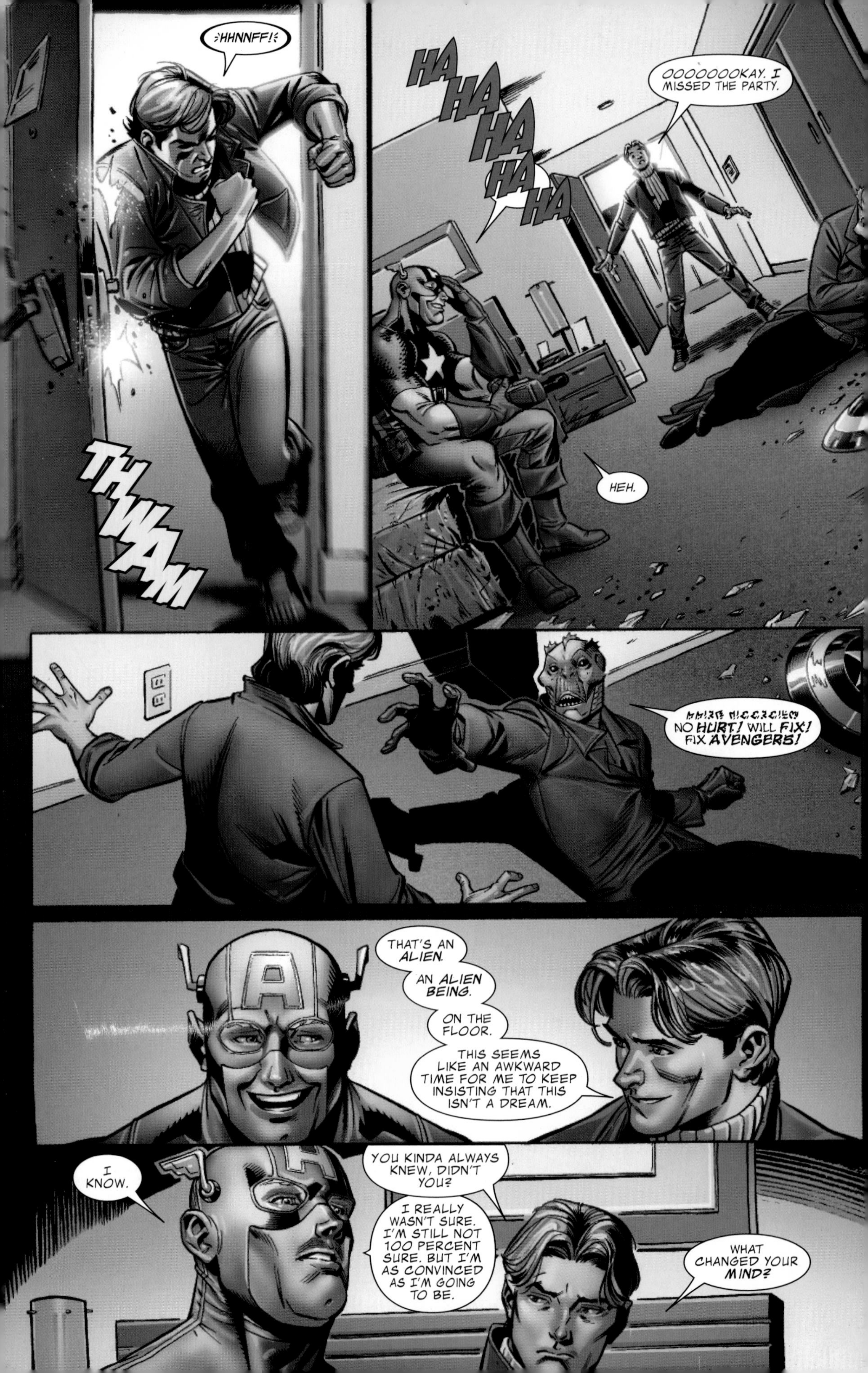
HHNNFF!
THWAM
HA HA HA HA HA HA
OOOOOOOKAY. I MISSED THE PARTY.
HEH.
NO HURT! WILL FIX! FIX AVENGERS!
THAT'S AN ALIEN.
AN ALIEN BEING.
ON THE FLOOR.
THIS SEEMS LIKE AN AWKWARD TIME FOR ME TO KEEP INSISTING THAT THIS ISN'T A DREAM.
I KNOW.
YOU KINDA ALWAYS KNEW, DIDN'T YOU?
I REALLY WASN'T SURE. I'M STILL NOT 100 PERCENT SURE. BUT I'M AS CONVINCED AS I'M GOING TO BE.
WHAT CHANGED YOUR MIND?

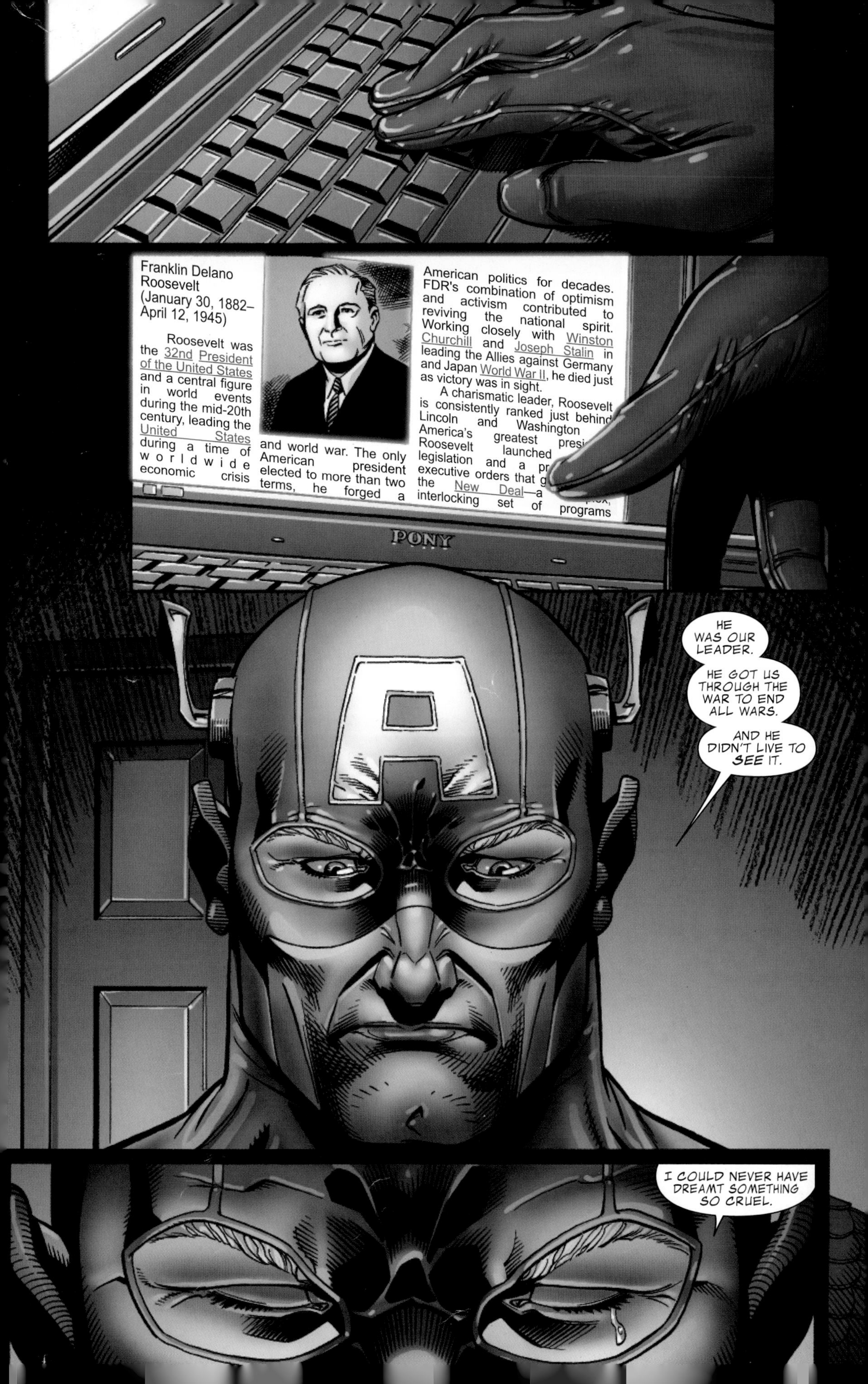

Franklin Delano Roosevelt (January 30, 1882–April 12, 1945)
Roosevelt was the 32nd President of the United States and a central figure in world events during the mid-20th century, leading the United States during a time of worldwide economic crisis and world war. The only American president elected to more than two terms, he forged a
American politics for decades. FDR's combination of optimism and activism contributed to reviving the national spirit. Working closely with Winston Churchill and Joseph Stalin in leading the Allies against Germany and Japan World War II, he died just as victory was in sight.
A charismatic leader, Roosevelt is consistently ranked just behind Lincoln and Washington America's greatest
Roosevelt launched
legislation and a
executive orders that
the New Deal—a
interlocking set of programs
PONY
HE WAS OUR LEADER.
HE GOT US THROUGH THE WAR TO END ALL WARS.
AND HE DIDN'T LIVE TO SEE IT.
I COULD NEVER HAVE DREAMT SOMETHING SO CRUEL.

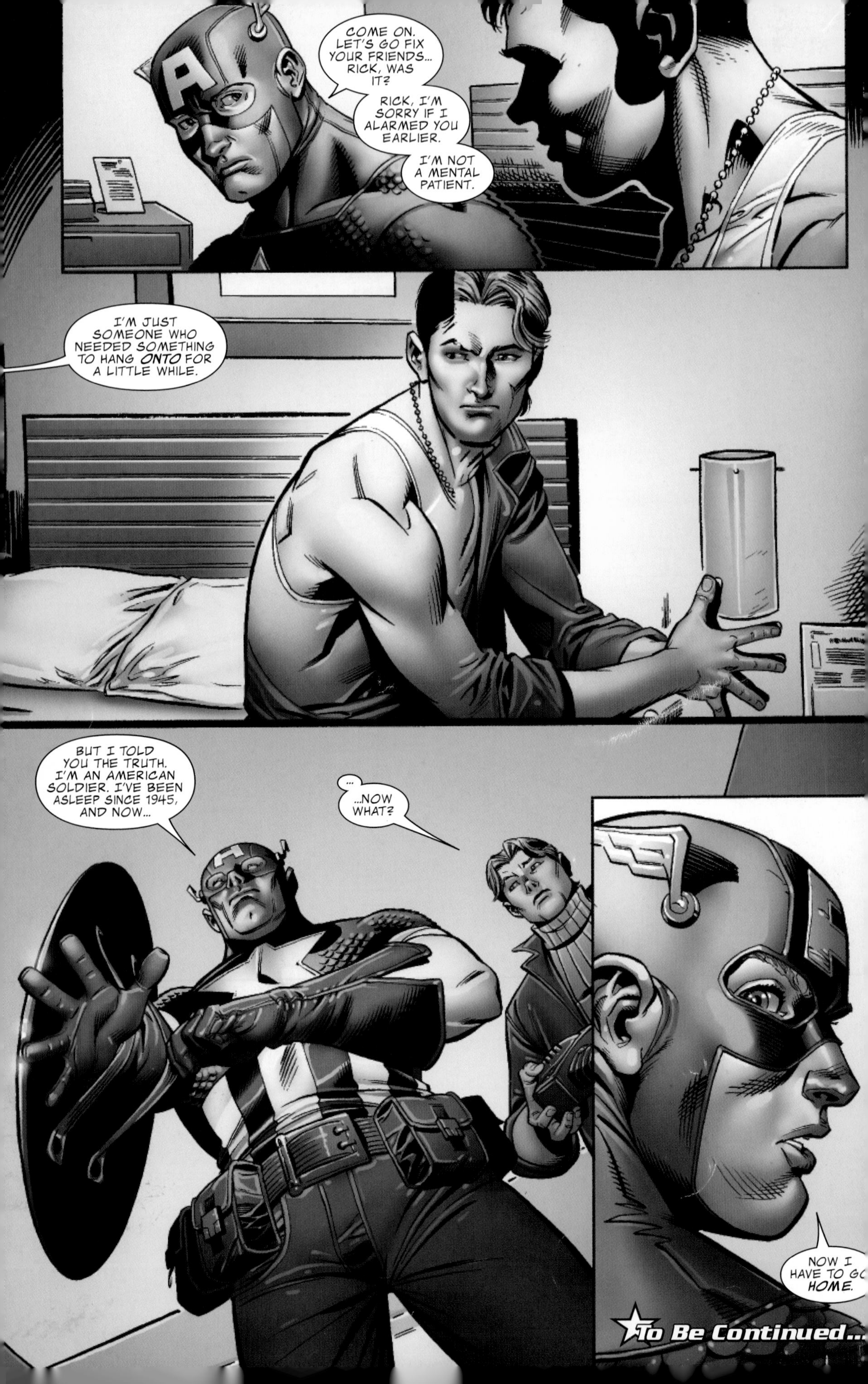
COME ON. LET'S GO FIX YOUR FRIENDS... RICK, WAS IT?
RICK, I'M SORRY IF I ALARMED YOU EARLIER.
I'M NOT A MENTAL PATIENT.
I'M JUST SOMEONE WHO NEEDED SOMETHING TO HANG ONTO FOR A LITTLE WHILE.
BUT I TOLD YOU THE TRUTH. I'M AN AMERICAN SOLDIER. I'VE BEEN ASLEEP SINCE 1945, AND NOW...
...
...NOW WHAT?
NOW I HAVE TO GO HOME.
To Be Continued...